FELI
CITA

The Octopus Escapes

Maile Meloy   pictures by Felicita Sala

putnam

G. P. Putnam's Sons

The octopus was happy in his cave.
He watched the world go by outside.

Bright fish darted by, some in schools and some alone.
He could see starfish from his door, and shiny mussels.

Sometimes waves came rolling in.
Little shivery ones,

or big tumbling ones.

The waves left sand on his
floor, so he swept it out.

Sometimes crabs came in. He liked
to chase them for dinner.

One day, something
new came into his cave.

He wrestled with it
and pulled it free.

It was empty, so he
climbed inside to hide.

But that was a mistake.

Then he was in a glass house that wasn't a cave.
The glass house was in a big room where a human peered in at him.
Behind her, there were sad gray sharks and slow sea stars
in glass houses of their own.

The human said, "He's shy,"
and gave him tests that looked like toys.
Sometimes the tests were hard,
and he felt smart.

But sometimes they were easy.

The human taught him to take pictures
of the people who came to see him.
People love to be in pictures.

They made funny faces.

But every day was the same in the glass house.
The food came at the same time.
It always tasted the same, and he didn't have
to chase it.

There were no waves. No little shivery ones.
No big tumbling ones.

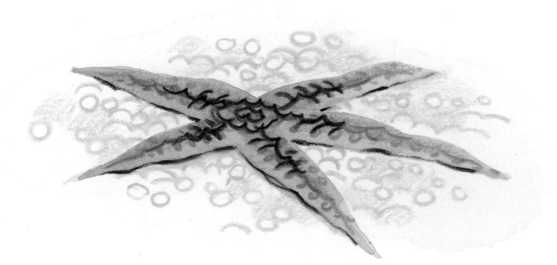

He missed the different fish swimming by his cave.
And the starfish and shiny mussels.

He missed warm spots in cold water, and cold spots in warm.
He hadn't known how nice that was until it was gone.

He tried to tell the
human he was bored.

He tried to show her how small the tank was.

But she only laughed and peeled
his tentacles off her arms—

one
    by one
by one
    by one
by one
    by one
by one
    by one.

That was when he knew he had to go.

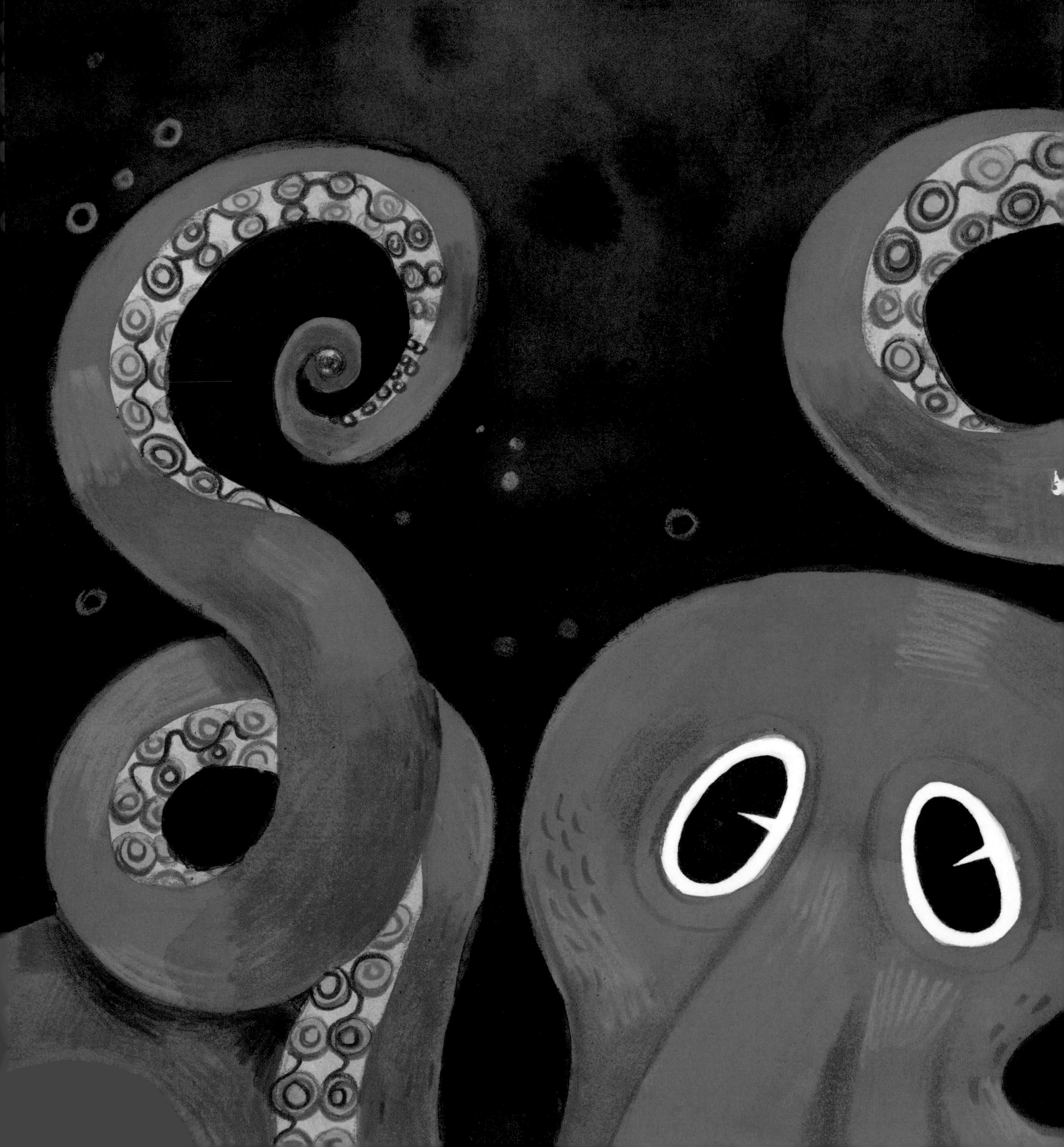

He waited for night to come.
The same old dinner plopped into the same still water.
The sleepy sharks cruised back and forth,
and the slow sea stars dozed.

The lights went out.

And it was time.

He took one more picture
so they wouldn't worry.

Then he slid down the glass
and across the floor.

He made himself flat and squeezed beneath the door.

Outside, the pier was noisy and bright.
But he smelled the salt of the ocean close by.
He reached way,

way,

way down,

until he felt the spray—
and dropped!

He changed colors three times in the water,
just because he could.

It was a long swim back to his cave.
The ocean was warm and cold and shivery and tumbling.
He had to dive away from boats.
And he got very hungry.

But he thought of the same food plopping into the tank.
And the same unchanging water.
And the four glass walls he couldn't swim through.

And he kept on, until he saw starfish
and mussels he knew.

At last, he found his cave.

He chased a crab and brought it home for dinner.
But there was sand on his floor.
And there were fish sleeping in his bed.
He swept them out—OUT!

He made his cave just right.
No one gave him tests or wanted a picture taken.

He was home, and he could do what he wanted.
And so he settled in to watch the world swim by.

For Lucile, Michael, and Caitlin —M.M.

For all the good people working for the
conservation of our oceans —F.S.

G. P. Putnam's Sons

An imprint of Penguin Random House LLC, New York

Visit us online at penguinrandomhouse.com

Library of Congress Cataloging-in-Publication Data
Names: Meloy, Maile, author. | Sala, Felicita, illustrator.
Title: The octopus escapes / Maile Meloy; illustrated by Felicita Sala.
Description: New York: G. P. Putnam's Sons, [2021] | Summary: "An octopus is taken from his undersea home
to live in an aquarium, but he soon tires of captive life"—Provided by publisher.
Identifiers: LCCN 2020034122 | ISBN 9781984812698 (hardcover) | ISBN 9781984812711 (kindle edition) |
ISBN 9781984812704 (epub) | Subjects: CYAC: Octopuses—Fiction. | Aquariums—Fiction.
Classification: LCC PZ7.M516354 Oc 2021 | DDC [E]—dc23
LC record available at https://lccn.loc.gov/2020034122

Manufactured in China by RR Donnelley Asia Printing Solutions Ltd.
ISBN 9781984812698
1   3   5   7   9   10   8   6   4   2

Design by Eileen Savage. Text set in Beorcana Micro Pro.
The art was done in gouache, watercolor, and pastels on paper.

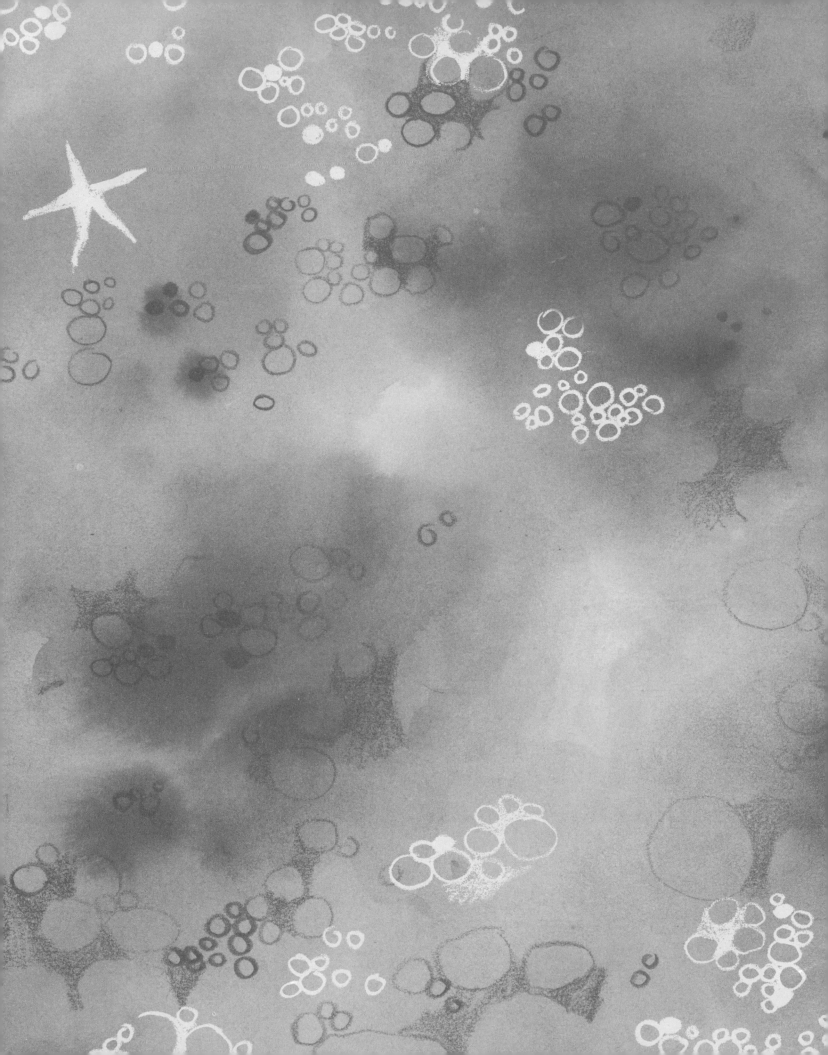